Invitations to Personal Reading
Curriculum Foundation Classroom Library
Scott, Foresman and Company

Realistic Stories	
Betsy's Little Star	Carolyn Haywood
Emmett's Pig	Mary Stolz
Mop Top	Don Freeman
Nobody Listens to Andrew	Elizabeth Guilfoile
A Pair of Red Clogs	Masako Matsuno

Animals —True and Imaginary	
Baby Elephant's Trunk	Sesyle Joslin
Little Black Puppy	Charlotte Zolotow
The No-Bark Dog	Stan Williamson
Seven Diving Ducks	Margaret Friskey
The Unhappy Hippopotamus	Nancy Moore

Fun and Fancy	
Four Fur Feet	Margaret Wise Brown
Georgie to the Rescue	Robert Bright
The Mitten	retold by Alvin Tresselt
No Fighting, No Biting!	Else Minarik
The Three Wishes	retold by Joseph Jacobs

Books to Enrich the Content Fields	
The Big Book of Real Building and Wrecking Machines	George Zaffo
Columbus	Ingri and Edgar d'Aulaire
Space Alphabet	Irene Zacks
What Is A Frog	Gene Darby
What's Inside?	May Garelick

Books Too Good to Miss	
Away We Go!	compiled by Catherine McEwen
Hide and Seek Fog	Alvin Tresselt
I Wish, I Wish	Lisl Weil
Inch by Inch	Leo Lionni
Otto in Africa	William Pène du Bois

BABY ELEPHANT'S TRUNK

BABY
ELEPHANT'S
TRUNK

BY SESYLE JOSLIN

PICTURES BY LEONARD WEISGARD

HARCOURT, BRACE & WORLD, INC., NEW YORK

Special Scott, Foresman and Company Edition
for the *Invitations to Personal Reading* Program

Also by Sesyle Joslin and Leonard Weisgard

BRAVE BABY ELEPHANT

This edition is printed and distributed by
Scott, Foresman and Company by special arrangement
with Harcourt, Brace & World, Inc.,
757 Third Avenue, New York, N. Y. 10017.

Pour
Father Elephant
avec amour

BABY ELEPHANT'S TRUNK

Hello, Mother Elephant," said Baby Elephant, coming into the house one evening.

"*Bonsoir,* Baby Elephant," said Mother Elephant.

"*Bonsoir?* What does *bonsoir* mean?"

"*Bonsoir* means good evening. It is French."

"Ah," said Baby Elephant. "I see." He took off his cap and bowed in a most elegant fashion. "*Bonsoir,* Mother Elephant," he said.

Baby Elephant went to the cupboard and very quickly ate a loaf of bread for his before-supper snack.

"Mother Elephant," said Baby Elephant, "I am wondering what *is* French?"

"French is the language that elephants who live in France speak."

"Of course," said Baby Elephant. "I see."

Baby Elephant went to the refrigerator and got out a pitcher of milk, which he drank in one rather large gulp.

"Mother Elephant," said Baby Elephant, "now I am wondering why are *we* speaking French?"

"Because we are going to cross the ocean and go to France for a visit."

"Hurrah!" said Baby Elephant. "We are going to cross the ocean and visit France! That is certainly fine news! Can you tell me, Mother Elephant, how to say hurrah in French?"

"*Certainement,* Baby Elephant. *Hourra* is the French word for hurrah."

Baby Elephant jumped up and down. He made a good bit of noise, as baby elephants will. *"Hourra!"* he said. *"Hourra! Hourra!"*

"A little less noise, *s'il vous plaît,"* said Mother Elephant, flapping her ears downward in an effort not to hear her son.

"Does *s'il vous plaît* mean please?"

Mother Elephant nodded her head.

"Aha!" said Baby Elephant. "That is just what I thought."

Baby Elephant went into the living room and came back wearing Grandmother Elephant's pince-nez and holding Father Elephant's pipe.

"Now, then, Mrs. Elephant," he said, in a voice not at all his own, "do you know how to say yes in French?"

"*Oui* is the way one says yes in French."

"Excellent, Mrs. Elephant. I am certainly glad you could answer that because I am thinking *oui* is the most important word for a mother elephant to know. Don't you agree?"

"*Oui*," said Mother Elephant.

Baby Elephant put down Father Elephant's pipe and took off Grandmother Elephant's pince-nez.

"*S'il vous plaît,* Mother Elephant, may I pack my trunk to go to France? I think I should pack my trunk right now, this minute. Don't you agree?"

"*Oui,*" said Mother Elephant.

"You are a very kind and agreeable mother elephant," Baby Elephant said.

"It is not hard," said Mother Elephant.

Baby Elephant hurried off to his room, but almost at once he called to his mother.

"Come look, Mother Elephant, *s'il vous plaît*. I have already got my trunk packed. *Hourra* for me!"

"What? You have already packed your trunk? *Vraiment!*" said Mother Elephant, very much surprised. She went quickly to Baby Elephant's room.

There was Baby Elephant standing next to his bed with his trunk curled up in a large suitcase. "You see, Mother Elephant, my trunk is really packed," and Baby Elephant snorted and trumpeted and could scarcely stand still, he was laughing so hard. He thought he had played an excellent joke on Mother Elephant.

"*Vraiment!*" snorted and trumpeted Mother Elephant. She too thought Baby Elephant had played an excellent joke on her.

"You are a *drôle* baby elephant and *je t'aime*," she said.

"Ho, I bet I know what that means," said Baby Elephant. "I bet *drôle* means funny and *je t'aime* means I love you."

"*C'est bien!*" said Mother Elephant. "That is just so, but how did you know?"

"Because," said Baby Elephant, "because that is what you always say. You always say to me, you are a funny baby elephant and I love you."

"Well, well," said Mother Elephant. "That is true. And now I shall help you really pack for our trip." Mother Elephant hustled about Baby Elephant's room collecting this and that, all the things a baby elephant would need in France.

"Now then," said Mother Elephant:

"la brosse à dents is the toothbrush,
le livre is the book,
le crayon is the pencil,
les pantoufles are the slippers,
le chapeau is the hat,
l'habit is the coat,
le pantalon are the trousers,
le parapluie is the umbrella,
and
l'ours is the bear."

"Well," said Baby Elephant, "I am certainly glad that you did not forget Bear because, after all, what would France be without him?"

"Not much," said Mother Elephant.

"Mother Elephant?"

"What is it?"

"Didn't you forget something? Didn't you forget to pack a hairbrush?"

"But you do not have a hairbrush because you do not have any hair. Did you forget that elephants have no hair? Did you forget that, my silly Baby Elephant?"

Baby Elephant was embarrassed, and he stood upon his head.

"Of course not," he said. But the truth was that, in all his excitement, he had quite forgotten that elephants have no hair.

"And now," said Mother Elephant, "it is time to eat your *souper*."

"*Souper* sounds like supper, and I am hoping it tastes like supper because I am very hungry," said Baby Elephant.

"*C'est bien!*" said Mother Elephant. "*Souper* does mean supper, and I shall tell you something else which very hungry baby elephants should know. *Merci* is the way to say thank you."

"*S'il vous plaît,* Mother Elephant, may I have some milk?"

"*Oui.* Here is *du lait.*"

"*Merci,* Mother Elephant.

"*S'il vous plaît,* Mother Elephant, may I have some bread?"

"*Oui.* Here is *du pain.*"

"*Merci,* Mother Elephant.

"*S'il vous plaît,* Mother Elephant, may I have some butter?"

"*Oui.* Here is *du beurre.*"

"*Merci,* Mother Elephant.

"*S'il vous plaît,* Mother Elephant, may I have some cake?"

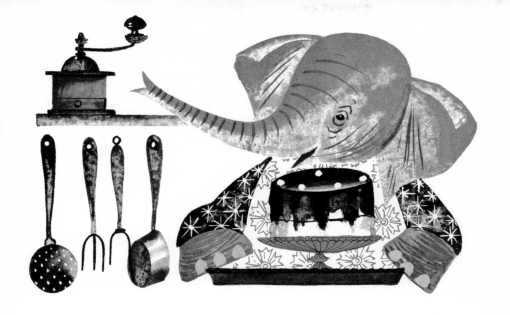

"*Non, non, non,* Baby Elephant. Not until you have finished *le lait, le pain,* and *le beurre.*"

"Now I am finished," said Baby Elephant.

"*C'est bien!*" said his mother. "Here is a cake for you. French elephants call it *gâteau.*"

"*Merci,* and so will I," said Baby Elephant. And he did. "Nice *gâteau,*" Baby Elephant said, "lovely *gâteau,* beautiful *gâteau.*"

"And now," said Mother Elephant, "it is time for bed."

"What, again?" said Baby Elephant.

"*Oui*. Again," said Mother Elephant.

"But I went to bed last night and the night before that and all the nights before that."

"That is true," said Mother Elephant. "And you will go to bed tonight and tomorrow night and all the nights after that."

"Oh, dear." Baby Elephant sighed. "Tell me, Mother Elephant, do French baby elephants have to go to bed?"

"*Certainement*. They go to sleep in a little *lit* just as you do."

"And do French mother elephants tell French baby elephants stories when they go to bed?" asked Baby Elephant as he got into his striped pajamas.

"*Oui*."

"Aha! That is just what I thought. Is it possible, Mother Elephant, that you could show me just *how* it is done?"

Mother Elephant snorted and trumpeted and shook all over with laughter.

"You are a *drôle* baby elephant and *je t'aime,*" she said. "All right, all right. I will tell you about our trip to France."

"*C'est bien!*" said Baby Elephant, and he curled up most contentedly in his bed.

"To begin with," said Mother Elephant, "we shall take a taxi to the pier and then we shall board our boat, which is called *bateau.*"

"Will it be a big *bateau?*"

"*Oui.* A *grand bateau.*"

"And will the *grand bateau* have a captain?"

"Oh, *oui, oui. Le grand bateau* will indeed have a *capitaine.*"

"*C'est bien!* And then what, Mother Elephant?"

"Why then we shall sail across *la mer.*"

"*Vraiment!* And then what, Mother Elephant?"

"Why then we shall go to *Paris,* which is a city of France. It is very beautiful, and there are *beaucoup de* French elephants and *beaucoup de* French people as well."

Baby Elephant suddenly sat up in bed. "Mother Elephant?"

"What is it?"

"I am thinking," said Baby Elephant, "I am thinking what should one do if one accidentally knocks down some small French person in *Paris?*"

"That is easy, Baby Elephant. One simply says *pardonnez-moi,* meaning pardon me."

"I will remember that. Just in case," said Baby Elephant.

"C'est bien!" said his mother.

"Tell me more about what we shall do, *s'il vous plaît.*"

"We shall go to *l'hôtel* and we shall unpack our trunks and you will put away:

    la brosse à dents
    le livre
    le crayon
    les pantoufles
    le chapeau
    l'habit
    le pantalon
    le parapluie
    and
    l'ours."

"C'est bien! And then what?"

"It is possible that we shall go to the circus, which is called *le cirque*, and to the park, which is called *le parc.*"

"*Hourra!*"

Baby Elephant suddenly sat up in bed. "Mother Elephant?"

"What is it?"

"I am thinking again," said Baby Elephant. "I am thinking what does one say if one is running fast in *le parc* and one falls down and hurts a knee?"

"That is easy, Baby Elephant. One simply says *zut!* meaning oh, gosh darn it!"

"*Zut!*" said Baby Elephant. "Oh my! *Zut* is certainly a fine word, and I might not even wait until I am in *le parc* in *Paris* to say *zut*, because, who knows, I might be hurting a knee almost anytime now."

"You will not be hurting a knee or anything else if you will go to sleep now."

"That is true, Mother Elephant, but I cannot go to sleep because you have not finished telling me what we shall do in *Paris.*"

"We shall have *souper. Du lait, du pain,* and *du beurre.*"

"And *le gâteau?*" asked Baby Elephant.

"*Oui.* When you finish *le lait, le pain,* and *le beurre,* then you may have *le gâteau.* I have heard of a *pâtisserie* which makes a French Elephant Holiday *gâteau* that is six feet high."

"*Vraiment!* And then?"

"Why, then I shall say that is all, *c'est tout,* and I shall ask you if you remembered to brush your teeth and you will say *certainement,* and then I shall tuck you in your *lit,* like this, and I shall give you a kiss, like this, and I shall say *bonne nuit, dors bien.*" And Mother Elephant began to tiptoe out of Baby Elephant's room.

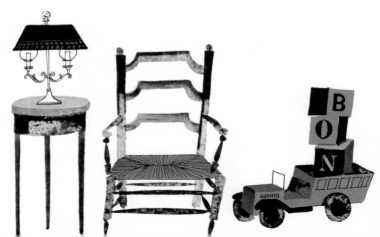

"Mother Elephant," called Baby Elephant.

"What is it?"

"I am thinking of something to tell you."

"What is it, Baby Elephant?"

"I forgot to brush my teeth."

"Well, you had better brush them then. *Tout de suite.*"

"*Oui*, Mother Elephant," and Baby Elephant hurried off to brush his teeth and hurried back into bed again.

"Is it possible, Mother Elephant, that you know how to say I want some water in French?"

"*Oui*. It is possible," said Mother Elephant. "*Je veux de l'eau.*"

"You are certainly clever, Mother Elephant."

"It is nice of you to say so, Baby Elephant."

"Mother Elephant?"

"What, again?" said Mother Elephant, flapping her ears in dismay. "What can it be now? I have told you a story and you have brushed your teeth. What is it you can possibly want now, Baby Elephant?"

"Je veux de l'eau," said Baby Elephant.

Mother Elephant brought Baby Elephant a glass of water.

"Merci," said Baby Elephant. "Do you know what I am going to do now, Mother Elephant?"

"Vraiment! What are you going to do now?"

"I am going to sleep. *Tout de suite.*"

"*Hourra!*" said Mother Elephant. "That is certainly fine news."

"*Bonne nuit,* Mother Elephant."

"*Bonne nuit,* Baby Elephant, *dors bien.*"

GLOSSARY

le bateau *(luh bah-toh')*—the boat
beaucoup de *(boh-koo' duh)*—many (of)
le beurre *(luh burr)*—the butter
bonne nuit *(bun nwee')*—good night
bonsoir *(bohn-swahr')*—good evening
la brosse à dents *(lah bross ah dahn)*—the toothbrush
le capitaine *(luh ka-pee-tayn')*—the captain
certainement *(sare-tayn-mohn')*—certainly
c'est bien *(say b-yen')*—that's good!
c'est tout *(say too')*—that's all
le chapeau *(luh sha-poh')*—the hat
le cirque *(luh seerk)*—the circus
le crayon *(luh kray-yohn')*—the pencil
dors bien *(dor b-yen')*—sleep well
drôle *(drohl)*—funny
du beurre *(doo burr)*—some butter
du lait *(doo lay)*—some milk
du pain *(doo pa-n)*—some bread
le gâteau *(luh gah-toh')*—the cake
grand *(grahn)*—large
l'habit *(lah-bee')*—the coat
l'hôtel *(low-tel')*—the hotel

hourra! *(oo-rah')*—hurrah!

je t'aime *(zhuh tem)*—I love you

je veux de l'eau *(zhuh vuh duh low)*—I want some water

le lait *(luh lay)*—the milk

le lit *(luh lee)*—the bed

le livre *(luh lee'-vr)*—the book

la mer *(lah mare)*—the sea

merci *(mare-see)*—thank you

non *(nohn)*—no

oui *(wee)*—yes

l'ours *(loorss)*—the bear

le pain *(luh pa-n)*—the bread

le pantalon *(luh pahn-ta-lohn')*—the trousers

les pantoufles *(lay pahn-too'-fl)*—the slippers

le parapluie *(luh para-plwee')*—the umbrella

le parc *(luh paark)*—the park

pardonnez-moi *(par-dun-nay-mwa')*—pardon me

Paris *(pah-ree')*—Paris

la pâtisserie *(lah pah-tees'-eree)*—the bakery shop

s'il vous plaît *(seel voo play)*—please

le souper *(luh soo-pay)*—the supper

tout de suite *(toot sweet)*—immediately

vraiment *(vray-mohn')*—really! indeed!

zut! *(zoot)*—oh, gosh darn it!